CARTOON NETWORK™

PASTE MAKES WASTE

Adapted by Laura Dower from
the "Paste Makes Waste" storyboards by Don Shank

Based on "THE POWERPUFF GIRLS," as
created by Craig McCracken

SCHOLASTIC INC.

New York   Toronto   London   Auckland   Sydney
Mexico City   New Delhi   Hong Kong

ISBN 0-439-19105-X

Special thanks to Jim Steck for cover and interior illustrations.

Cover designed by Peter Koblish
Interiors designed by Mary Hall

12 11 10 9 8 7 6 5 4 3 2 1   0 1 2 3 4 5/0

Printed in the U.S.A.
First Scholastic printing, October 2000

The city of Townsville!
And just outside the city limits — Pokey Oaks County!
And smack-dab in the middle of this sleepy suburb — Pokey Oaks
Kindergarten! Come on in!

Ms. Keane had an important announcement.

"All right, kids. Continue working on your projects. It's time for roll call."

Ms. Keane read each name aloud.

"Julie . . . Julie Bean?" *"Here!"*

"Harry . . . Harry Pit?" *"Here!"*

"Blossom? Bubbles? Buttercup?" *"Present!" "Here!" "Yup!"*

"Lloyd Floijoidson?" *"Huh?"*
"Floyd Floijoidson?" *"Wha?"*
"Mitchell . . . Mitchell Mitchelson?" *"It's Mitch! Yeah, I'm here. OK?"*
Finally, she read the last name on her list.
"Elmer . . . Elmer Sglue?"

"Heeeere . . ."

Poor Elmer Sglue.
He liked to eat paste
and kids picked on him.

6

PASTE EATER! EEEEEEEW!

"Paste eater! Eeeeeew!" screeched Mitch Mitchelson. Mitch shoved Elmer's chair back and sent him flopping to the floor in a gummy heap. Then he dunked a Popsicle-stick man into more paste and plopped *that* (splat!) right onto Elmer's head.

The kids wailed with laughter . . . even Buttercup.

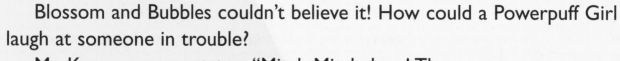

Blossom and Bubbles couldn't believe it! How could a Powerpuff Girl laugh at someone in trouble?

Ms. Keane was upset, too. "Mitch Mitchelson! That was a terrible thing to do! Children, you *must* behave!"

But the kids didn't listen.

Buttercup bobbed back and forth while her classmates called Elmer nasty names. She loved it!

Wow! Buttercup thought. This was *fun*! Yeah! Paste eaters deserved to be teased . . . and taunted . . . and terrorized! Yeah!

In a flash of green, Buttercup leaped onto the table . . . scooped up a pile of sticks and glue . . . and pointed a finger at Elmer Sglue.

"Hey, YOU!"

All at once, she scooped up some paste. . . .

9

Pow!

"Eat THIS, paste eater!" Buttercup screamed, hurling her handful of glue right at Elmer's head.

Sploooch!

Direct hit!

"Wa-wa-waaaaah!" Elmer cried, his face white with goo.

Yes, the paste eater was bawling like a baby.

Ms. Keane groaned. Blossom and Bubbles grimaced. And the rest of the kids pointed. . . .

"Ooooh! You're in trouble now!" they called to Buttercup.

"Whoops," Buttercup muttered. She *was* in trouble now. BIG trouble.

"Buttercup! Apologize right this instant!" cried Ms. Keane.

"Um . . . well . . . Elmer . . . I'm . . ." Buttercup blubbered. "I'm, uh . . . I'm . . . well . . . why did you have to . . . I mean . . ."

The other kids giggled. Buttercup glared at them.

"Er . . . doncha see, Elmer? I'm ssso . . . I am so . . . sssssoooooo . . ." But no matter how hard she tried, Buttercup just couldn't get the words out. "I'm so so sooooo . . . awwww, Elmer . . . you shoulda DUCKED!"

Brrriiing! The class bell rang.

"Whoo-hoo! Recess!" Mitch shrieked, and everyone in class dashed outside.

Ms. Keane leaned over Elmer to wipe the paste off his face.

"I'll deal with her later, Elmer dear. For now, let's get you cleaned up.
What those kids did was wrong . . . but, you know, it isn't good to eat paste."

"Why?" Elmer asked.

"Now, you just go outside and play with your friends," said Ms. Keane.
She pushed him gently toward the playground.

Outside on the playground, Blossom turned to her sister Buttercup. "That was really mean!"

"You should apologize," Bubbles added.

"Why?" Buttercup snorted. "He's just a dumb paste eater."

Elmer walked over to the farthest, safest spot in the playground, where no one could torture him. He sat under a tall tree and pulled out a jar of paste he had been hiding in his pocket.

"Stupid Mitch! Stupid Buttercup! She thinks she's all cool . . . just because *she* has superpowers. . . ." Elmer reached into his jar for a scoop of goop . . . and ate it. "*I* could be cool, too . . ." he continued, gulping glue as he muttered to himself, "if *I* had superpowers."

Meanwhile, on the other side of Townsville, there was an accident at the Marshmallow Charms factory! A simple cereal spill turned into a toxic terror! And somehow, someway, Elmer Sglue was affected by it!

A lab guy dropped some testing goo . . . then realized it was *toxic* — ooooh!
He wiped it up with a gooey rag . . . that ended up in a garbage bag . . .
That fell into a trashy truck . . . where a fly landed in the muck . . .
Grew extra legs and extra wings . . . extra eyes and other things . . .
The mutant bug just flew and flew . . . and what else did that superfly do?

TOXIC DUMP

RECYCLE WHITE PAPER ONLY!

17

"Hey, get up, Elmer!" Mitch Mitchelson barked.

"Yeah, get up! Yeah, get up!" Lloyd and Floyd Floijoidson chimed together.

Elmer got up, but Mitch just pushed him right back down.

"Hey, paste eater, I said GET UP!"

Elmer tried to stand again, but Mitch knocked him down again.

Across the playground, Buttercup grinned. "Elmer will never learn!"

What no one noticed, in the middle of all the pushing and shoving, was that pasty-faced Elmer was *changing*.

The next time he hit Elmer, Mitch got a little goo stuck on his thumb.

"Hey, man, what *is* this?" Mitch yelled, waving his hand in the air. "Hey, man, is this some kind of *snot*?"

Lloyd and Floyd laughed . . . but not for long. They looked up and saw . . .

. . . A giant shadow. Elmer. Growing.

Elmer Sglue was changing into something gooey . . . something goopy . . . something GIGANTIC!

"Dude! Dude!" cried Lloyd and Floyd, trying to get Mitch's attention.

Mitch looked up in terror. "Eeew, you're *gross*!" he yelped.

Elmer was now an enormous, white paste monster. He towered over Pokey Oaks Kindergarten. He was bubbling with goo. He could make it rain . . . GLUE!

The kids of Pokey Oaks panicked! What could *they* do?

This was a job for . . . The Powerpuff Girls!

Elmer squashed Mitch, Lloyd, Floyd, and seven other kids onto his sticky fingertips.

"Hey, you!" he screamed, wiggling his fingers. "Big bully, huh? Who's laughing now?"

He flicked the kids into the air, one by one. That's when Buttercup got mad. "Not so fast, paste eater!"

"Huh?" Elmer turned toward the show-off Powerpuff Girl and growled. That bossy Buttercup made him so mad his glue started *boiling*!

Elmer swatted Buttercup, smashing her into the school wall. *Splotch!*

"Whoa!" Buttercup moaned. "Blossom and Bubbles, ya gotta help me!"

"No way!" said Blossom. "You deserve what you get for picking on poor little Elmer."

Then The Powerpuff Girls heard a scream. Ms. Keane?! With a single swipe, Elmer had superglued their teacher to the school wall.

"He's gone crazy!" Blossom and Bubbles cried out, blasting into the air.

But it was too late. Elmer punched the other two Powerpuffs into the wall, too. Now *everyone* was stuck.

Ms. Keane screamed, "He's headed toward the city! You've got to stop him!"

"B-b-but we're hot-glued to a brick wall," squeaked Bubbles.

"That's IT!" yelled Buttercup. "Heat!" She shot heat rays from her eyes — and the glue dried up and cracked away lickety-split. "C'mon! Let's stick it to him!" Buttercup squawked.

With each gooey step, Elmer pounded a path of destruction through Townsville. He had people, cars, and even school buses *powerless* in his pasty paws.

Blossom, Bubbles, and Buttercup flew full speed ahead toward the paste monster. But wait! He was holding up a bus to block the way!

"Watch out! Swerve!" Blossom shrieked.

Blossom and Bubbles swerved in time, but Buttercup smash-landed a few feet away.

Blossom snarled, "That's it, Elmer! Now you've done it! Blood is thicker than glue!" She and Bubbles blasted off again.

But no sooner had the two Powerpuff Girls taken off when they got trapped in Elmer's tacky torso!

"Augh! I'm stuck!" Blossom cried.

"Augh! Me too!" Bubbles cried.

The sisters were sinking fast. *Who* would save them? Who would save Townsville?

Buttercup shook off her stars and jumped up.
"Okay, pasty face! You're gonna get socked in the kisser!"
Her sisters screamed out together, "No! You'll just get stuck!"
"You *know* what you have to do!" said Blossom.
"No!" said Buttercup. "I can fight him!" she blurted, and blazed into the air again. . . .

Could Buttercup destroy glue boy with her superpowers? She had to think fast. . . .

Zing! Buttercup had a brainstorm. She needed . . . flour! She found a sack of the white stuff and rolled around in it.

"Ha! I'm flour! You're glue! Try to fight an' I won't stick to you!"

Covered in flour, she blasted into the monster — but didn't even make a dent! In fact, she came out the other side!

Oh, no! Was Buttercup *beaten?*

"Buttercup! You *know* what to do! Butterc —" Blossom gurgled and was swallowed up at last by Elmer's goo.

"No! No! No!" Buttercup shouted. "Oh, all right! Er . . . Elmer? Uh . . . I . . . I'm ssss . . . I am sor . . . ssoorr . . . aw . . . rr . . . reeee!"

Elmer stopped dead in his gluey tracks. "Wh-wh-what?"

"I'm sorry I picked on you . . . and . . . that I called you a paste eater. . . ."

Elmer sniffled. "Thanks, Buttercup. Gee, that's all I ever wanted." He took Blossom and Bubbles out of his sticky body and placed them back on the ground.

Elmer and the Girls glued the sleepy suburb of Pokey Oaks back together. "Thanks for helping, Elmer," Buttercup said.

"Buttercup . . . you're cool," Elmer whispered.

"Yeah," Buttercup whispered back, "let's stick together!"

So once again, the day was saved, thanks to The Powerpuff Girls!